Crane Crossing

KLaSKY CSUPO INC.

Based on the TV series *The Wild Thornberrys*® created by Klasky Csupo, Inc. as seen on Nickelodeon®

SIMON SPOTLIGHT
An imprint of Simon & Schuster Children's Publishing Division
1230 Avenue of the Americas, New York, New York 10020

Manufactured in the United States of America

First Edition
2 4 6 8 10 9 7 5 3 1

ISBN 0-689-84780-7

Library of Congress Control Number 2001098576

Crane Crossing

by Mark Dubowski
illustrated by Jim Durk

Simon Spotlight/Nickelodeon

New York   London   Toronto   Sydney   Singapore

Introduction

What do you get when you cross an airplane with a tricycle?

It's called an ultralight. My mom and I were flying in one, high above the ground.

"Look out for the top of that tree!" I shouted.

"No problem!" she yelled back.

I would have been scared to death if she hadn't been acting so brave. Mom says when you're brave it rubs off on others, and I guess she's right.

Mom and I leaned to the left, and she pushed the control bar sideways to the right. It was like turning a sled . . .

arounnnnd we went! On the other side we leaned left again until we were straight up and down. We made it! Then . . .

"Mom, look out for the water tower!" I yelled.

Mom pulled back on the control bar, and we climbed over it like a roller coaster. Higher, higher, higher, and we were over it!

We were flying over a Texas ranch, following a barbwire fence that looked like toothpicks on a string from where we were. I was on the lookout for our landing strip, which was really just a dirt road in a wheat field next to an old barn that our flying teacher called Ultralight International Airport. His name is Dr. Dave Hatcher. He is called "doctor" because, besides being a flying instructor, he is a biologist. People call him "Doc."

My mom and dad knew him from the research he was doing with whooping cranes. Whooping cranes are the tallest bird

in North America—an adult is almost as tall as my dad. There used to be thousands of them, but they're almost extinct. Dr. Hatcher was one of many scientists working to bring them back. My mom and dad were planning to film a show about his work.

Doc owned two ultralights, which he used in working with cranes. He called them sky trikes. Trike is short for tricycle, of course.

"Good luck, Mom!" I said. She was taking the final test for her pilot's license—a "solo" trip to prove that she could operate the plane on her own. I saw Doc down on the ground, watching us come in. He was writing something on a clipboard he was holding. It was Mom's scores. My dad had already passed his test. I saw him standing next to Doc, cheering us on. He could talk to us by two-way radio.

"Mosquito 1 coming in for a landing," my mom said.

"Ground to Mosquito 1. We read you loud and clear," my dad said back. "Welcome home."

Mom pushed the control stick forward and the ultralight dropped a few feet. I heard a whirring noise above her head. She was wearing a special helmet with a camera mounted on top. She'd just turned it on to film her landing.

I noticed, though, that we had a slight problem. I was looking at some cows grazing in one of Doc's fields. There was a trick Doc had taught us about telling the wind direction from the way the cows were standing. Almost always, they graze with the wind blowing from behind. Doc called it the Cow Rule: "You can tell which way the wind blows by looking at a cow's nose!"

"Turn around, Mom!" I shouted. "The wind is going the other way." She was flying with the wind at our backs. Coming in the other way would make a better landing, straight into the wind. A headwind would give us lift. It would turn our trike into a glider when the engine slowed down for landing. We circled around in time and came in from the other direction. As we glided down we cruised over a big animal pen. Seven white birds watched us from inside the fence.

They were whooping cranes, the reason we were here.

Chapter 1

"Congratulations," Doc said. "You're a pilot!"

Mom's perfect landing meant she aced her test. "Awesome!" I said.

"Smashing!" said my dad.

"It almost was!" Mom said. "Who put that tree in the way?"

Doc smiled. "That particular tree has a name, you know. We call it the Green Cloud. Remember the rule: When clouds abound, go around." Doc had a rule for everything. If there wasn't one already, he made one up. The Cloud Rule went for all kinds of clouds, even the white fluffy ones.

Trike pilots try to stick to where they can see clearly, which is definitely not inside a cloud.

"Jolly good!" my dad said. "I suppose that means Marianne passed her pilot's examination with flying colors! Get it? Green cloud? Flying colors?"

My dad can be a little corny sometimes.

Doc pulled two wallet-size cards from under the spring on his clipboard and held them up for Mom and Dad to see. "As your instructor," he said, "I'm proud to present you, Marianne, and you, Nigel, with your pilot's wings." He handed them to my mom and dad.

Dad got a dreamy look on his face, and I felt a speech coming on.

"I'd like to thank my flight instructor, my family, and the entire state of Texas for making this possible," he said.

Mom laughed. "Hush, Nigel," she said. "It's not the Academy Awards, you know."

My dad's eyes lit up. "What a brilliant thought! I can see it now! Hollywood! May I have the envelope, please . . . yes! YES! The winner for Best Documentary: *The Great Whooping Crane Adventure,* starring Nigel Thornberry, filmed by Marianne Thornberry!"

There went my dad's extra-large imagination.

"Everyone stands," he continues, "and cheers as I raise the Oscar for the cameras!"

"Ow, Dad," I said. "That's not the Oscar, that's my pigtail."

"Sorry, poppet," he said, letting go of my braid. "I suppose I got a little carried away there. Ahem."

The movie my dad was dreaming about was the one my mom was going to be shooting over the next couple of weeks. The stars of it, besides my dad, were the whooping cranes we flew over in the trike.

Whooping cranes are an endangered species, and the ones in Doc's pen were hatched and raised on his ranch as part of a project to make sure they didn't become extinct. The cranes are easy to raise when they're chicks. You just feed them.

When they get older, though, it starts to get interesting. A whooping crane learns everything it knows from its mom and dad—including how to migrate. In other words, where they should go to live in the winter and the summer.

Well, those pen-raised cranes of Doc didn't have a whooping crane mom and dad. The only parent they had was Doc. He tried to make up for it—when he fed them, he wore a hand puppet that looked like the head of a whooping crane.

But now he had his biggest job coming up as a whooping crane parent: teaching his birds how to migrate.

Together, in the ultralights, we were all going to lead Doc's cranes on their migration route, all the way from Texas, where they had been living all winter, to a safe place in Canada for the summer.

"Look at those cranes," Doc said. Two of them in the pen were standing face-to-face with wings spread like fans. One of them crouched, then hopped straight up and landed again in the same spot. Then the other one did the same thing.

"They're dancing," I said.

"That breeze coming out of the south is a message to them that it's time to get going," Doc said. "They're getting ready to go south for the summer and start a family."

My sister, Debbie, walked over. "He means it's time to move to their summer home and lay a big fat egg," she muttered. She glowered at the dancing cranes. "Dumb dodos."

"They're not dodos," I told her. Dodos

were extinct. "Now, stop being mean."

Debbie had been crabby ever since she'd seen the ultralights. It wasn't the flying she minded. It was the helmet. Wearing a helmet made a dent in her hair.

"Chin up, Deborah," said my dad. "We're all going to have a smashing . . ."—he glanced over at the ultralights—"I mean, a lovely time." Debbie felt better when Dad announced our seat assignments for the first day. Doc would be going up in one trike. Dad and I would fly the other. Everyone else would ride in the Commvee—Mom, Debbie, Darwin, and Donnie. We'd take turns along the way.

"I've got our rest stops all mapped out," Doc said. He showed us his map case. "Remember the rule: A map at any cost is better than getting lost."

Debbie rolled her eyes.

I, on the other hand, couldn't wait to get started.

Chapter 2

It was still dark and everyone else was still sleeping when I left the Commvee to check on the whooping cranes one more time before leaving. On the way out I taped the bumper sticker I made onto the Commvee. It said CRANE CROSSING, under a picture of a whooping crane in flight.

We'd only been staying with Doc for a week, and I was already the best—besides Doc, of course—at picking the birds out and knowing their names. There was Snowman and Lightning, Salt and Pepper, Zoom, Popcorn, and my favorite, Maggie. She had been the last to hatch. Doc said she'd been last in line ever since.

I didn't care—she was still my favorite. I wasn't sure why. Maybe because she seemed like she needed a friend more than the other birds.

It was kind of funny, but in a way, I knew Maggie even better than Doc did. That was because I could talk to her—really talk to her.

Ever since that African shaman gave me the gift of gab, I've had the ability to talk to any kind of animal. I keep it a secret, though. The shaman warned me that if I told another person, I would break the spell. I have no idea how it works—I just do it. Darwin's the only one in my family who knows. Because he's a chimpanzee, not a person, he can know my secret.

"Good morning, Maggie," I said. We'd talked many times before, so she wasn't surprised.

"Hi, Eliza," she said. I noticed she didn't sound very happy.

"You should be excited," I said. "You're going on a big trip today!" Doc had been practicing with Maggie and the other birds for weeks, teaching them to follow the ultralights. Now every time he let them follow a trike up, they lined up behind it in a perfect V.

"I'm a little nervous about the trip, actually," said Maggie.

"Don't be silly," I said. "You'll have a great time! Take it from me, I'm an expert when it comes to travel. You'll love it." Seeing new places is something my family does all the time.

"But . . ." She didn't have to finish what she was saying. I knew what she was thinking. The look in her eyes told me she was scared.

"Don't worry about a thing," I told her. None of the birds in Doc's pen had been away from home before. "All your friends are coming. It's their first trip too." I tried one of Doc's tricks. "Remember the rule: When it's spring, going north is your thing."

Maggie blinked. I could tell I wasn't getting through to her. "Just trust me," I said. "I've been traveling all my life, and every day is a blast."

Maggie looked down and shook her head. "I couldn't imagine leaving this place," she said. "It's all I've ever known."

"I'll be there with you," I told her. "I won't let anything happen to you. Promise!" I reached out my hand, Maggie put her foot in it, and we shook on it.

The cranes all knew it was time to go. They didn't need anyone to tell them; they could just feel it in the wind. Everyone except Maggie seemed really excited too. If they had mom and dad cranes to show them the way, I knew they'd already be halfway to Canada.

Someone was in the doorway behind me. I turned around and saw Darwin.

"You look as worried as Maggie," I told him. "It must be contagious."

"I'm concerned about the flying, Eliza," he said. "You're not a bird, you know. Humans weren't made for flying."

"That's sweet, Darwin," I said. "But you don't have to worry about me. And so what if humans weren't made for flying? That's what the trike is for."

"What you're about to do is dangerous," he told me.

"I'll be careful," I told him. "And remember, if there is a problem, we can always land. With or without the engine." Without the propeller running, an ultralight turns into a glider. It can't go any higher, but it can still go in for a landing.

I heard engines starting up outside the barn. It was time to go. My dad was out on the runway with his trike engine running. I pulled on a helmet and climbed in behind him. The pilot rides in front, the passenger rides in back. I sat down in a bucket seat that was a little higher than Dad's, which gave me a good view over the top of his head.

"Say 'cheese'!" Mom yelled from behind a camera. She was filming our takeoff.

Doc let the cranes out. They marched behind him as he headed for his trike. He started the propeller and climbed in. Mom revved up the Commvee, and Debbie put on her usual pouty face.

So what is it like to speed down a grassy strip with the wind in your hair and lift off the ground like a giant bird? Fun? Scary? The answer to both questions is a big yes!

"Here we go, boodle-de-doopkins," my dad said. He was pulling back on the control stick. The bumpy ride along the runway turned into a floaty feeling as we left the ground. I looked back and saw Doc zipping down the runway behind us, with the birds running behind him. All at once the birds spread their wings, his trike took off, and the whole flock rose into the air.

"Here they come!" I shouted. Dad looked over his shoulder. The cranes made a perfect V-pattern over Doc's wing. Dad cut our engine speed to let them pass and gave us a better view. It was so cool! The cranes beat their wings to pick up speed and then zoom—they glided along at forty miles an hour without even trying!

"They look like a painting!" I told my dad. There they were: Snowman, Lightning, Salt, Pepper, Zoom, Popcorn, and good old you-know-who in back—Maggie. It was going to be a long trip for her. We had over two thousand miles to go, three long weeks of flying.

Our goal for the first day was to make it to Oklahoma. Doc had picked out a couple of places where we could land, depending on how far we got. We got pretty far—150 miles to be exact.

Finally Doc spotted the farm he was looking for and descended. Our cranes were ready for a break. We landed on a deserted blacktop road and taxied off onto the dirt-road entrance to a farm where we had permission to spend the night.

Dad climbed out of our plane and used a cell phone to call mom in the Commvee to tell her we landed and give her our exact location. Doc walked the cranes over to a creek where they could cool off and have something to eat.

When the Commvee arrived, Darwin was the first to hop out. He rushed over to me. It was pretty clear to me he had something important to tell me, so we walked over to some trees behind the Commvee.

"I changed my mind about flying," he said.

"I told you," I said. "It's not so . . ."

"Dangerous?" Darwin said. "Oh, no, I still believe it's highly dangerous."

"Well, then?"

"It's just *more* dangerous to ride in the Commvee with Debbie behind the wheel. Please take me with you into the sky."

I laughed. "I don't think I can get you a seat on the ultralight," I said. "What are you talking about, anyway?"

"Debbie has a learner's permit to drive, you know."

Yikes. I forgot about that. "Mom actually let her drive?"

"For five minutes. We were on a back road. It seemed totally deserted! But it wasn't. . . ."

Uh-oh. I looked at the Commvee. It seemed fine.

"The other car was turning left, and we were turning right. It was one of those situations where . . . anyway, there was a close call and quite a bit of horn blowing."

"Well, that doesn't sound too bad," I said. "At least nobody got hurt."

"Oh, it was fine, up until Debbie got out to have a word with the other driver."

"Uh-oh."

"You can imagine. Have you ever heard of Colonel Coyote's Endangered Species Museum?"

"Colonel what?"

"I'm not making this up," Darwin said. "Colonel Coyote's Endangered Species Museum. Colonel Coyote himself was at the wheel. It's a large truck with all sorts of advertising painted on the sides. SEE THE SPOTTED OWL. PET THE MINK. FEED THE TREE FROG. He has this really mean dog with him too. He calls it Boo Boo. Anyway, Debbie got out and started complaining about his driving. Then your mother got out to investigate his vehicle, and she gave him a lecture about exploiting endangered animals for personal profit. The dog was barking and snarling at everybody the whole time."

"He's got real endangered animals with him?" I said.

"In the truck," Darwin said. "A spotted owl, a mink, and a tree frog. He drives around to shopping centers and sets up in the parking lots like a circus sideshow. Most unsavory. Says he does it all in the name of education, of course."

"That's terrible," I said. "He probably could get fined for keeping those animals cooped up in cages."

"That's the advantage of being mobile," Darwin said. "By the time the authorities hear about him, he's already in the next state. The bad news is, he spotted your CRANE CROSSING bumper sticker on the Commvee, and I think it gave him an idea. I wouldn't be surprised to see him try and add a whooping crane to the act."

"He's not getting any of our birds," I told Darwin.

"Let's hope not," he said. "But beware. I don't think we've seen the last of him."

Frankly, I wasn't too worried. Our camp was in the middle of nowhere. Miles and miles of open prairie surrounded us. Who could ever find us?

"Come on," I told Darwin, "let's go down to the creek and have a look at the cranes."

The creek Doc had picked out was beautiful. There was shade, and soft grass growing along the banks. The birds looked tired but happy, splashing around in the water. All except Maggie, that is. She seemed tired and sad.

"Everything okay, Maggie?" I said. I knew the answer before she opened her beak.

"Not really."

"What's the matter?"

"Texas is the matter," she said. "I miss it."

I gave her a pat on the shoulder, but I wasn't sure what I could say to make her feel better. "Hey, I know," I attempted, "why don't you think of this as your summer vacation? You're going up to Canada. The weather will be nice and cool. There'll be lots of new cranes to meet too. One of these days you might even start a family and have a little chick. Wouldn't that be fun?"

She thought about that for a minute. "Maybe," she said. "But I'll miss Texas."

"You might feel better after you see Canada. Hang in there," I said, hoping I was right, and gave her a wing a little squeeze.

Darwin and I climbed the bank and headed back for camp. We were amazed to discover that the quiet dirt road where the ultralights had landed had become an actual traffic jam! A crowd of people surrounded Mom and Dad. And I had thought we were in the middle of nowhere.

It was the ultralights—people had seen them and were curious. With candy-striped wings on the ultralights, I guess we were asking for attention. Plus my TV-star dad was there. Our camp had turned into an autograph party. He was happy to answer questions, but I noticed he wasn't telling anyone where our cranes were. The traffic jam made me think again about Colonel Coyote not being able to find us. If all these people could, why couldn't he?

After everyone was gone, Doc said from then on, we were going to hide the planes at night.

After dinner I helped Mom clean up the

dishes—it was one of the best ways I knew to have a talk with her.

"Have you noticed one of the birds acting a little, uh, sad?" I asked.

"As a matter of fact, I think I have," she said. "Is it the one called Maggie?"

"You got it," I said.

"I thought so. She doesn't look sick, though. Doc would know if she wasn't feeling well. It's more like she has the blues. I wonder . . ."

"What?"

"I wonder if she's homesick," Mom said.

Homesick?

I never would have thought of that. Can birds get homesick? I wondered. Come to think of it, have I ever been homesick? If I have, I don't remember.

"What's it feel like to be homesick?" I asked my mom.

She smiled. "That's a good question," she said, thinking. "It's hard to explain."

I put a dinner plate up on the shelf. "Maggie doesn't seem *sick,* exactly . . . ," I said.

"Right," Mom answered. "It's not that kind of sick. It's more about a sad, scared, or worried feeling that you miss home and wish you could go back there, right away."

"Maggie is going back to Texas," I said. "In the fall."

"I know," Mom said. "But homesickness feels like you can't wait. Maybe it's because you're worried something will change while you're away." Mom smiled. "But don't worry, it's perfectly normal. Everybody gets homesick at one time or another."

"Everybody?" I said.

"Everybody," Mom said.

Now I was worried. The way Mom explained homesickness, I was pretty sure I'd never had it, even though I was always leaving someplace behind. Not that I hadn't missed things about our home; it's just that the Commvee was home to me too.

Suddenly I wanted to be homesick. How could I help her if I didn't really understand how she was feeling?

Or maybe I wanted to be homesick because Mom had said it was "normal."

I felt strange enough already, walking around with the ability to talk to animals. The last thing I needed was another thing about me that was weird!

Chapter 3

We'd been flying for over a week. We were making over a hundred miles a day, riding a steady tailwind out of the south. It had carried us all the way across Kansas and Nebraska. South Dakota and Montana were coming up next. After that, we'd be in Canada.

In the old days our cranes might have stopped already. Back when there weren't so many farms, the country we'd been flying over had creeks everywhere. Beavers had dammed the creeks and made ponds. Cranes liked ponds as nesting places. They could find them all over the West.

It wasn't that way anymore. For cranes going north, there weren't a lot of ponds and lakes left for temporary rest stops. Instead of wild places, the resting areas we'd been using were on farms and ranches. Our cranes needed a lot of cooperation from people who lived along the migration route. They needed them to leave farm ponds filled with water and set aside places called wildlife sanctuaries, where no houses could be built, so migrating birds had safe places to spend the night.

All kinds of birds migrate, not just cranes. Anybody can give them a helping hand just by keeping a backyard bird feeder full in the spring and fall.

But how was I supposed to give a helping hand to a bird that was homesick?

At ten o'clock the next morning, with Doc in one ultralight, my mom and I in the other, and the whoopers behind us, we were cruising over a desert area in South Dakota called the Badlands, right next door to a mountain range called the Black Hills. Everybody was glad to see the Black Hills because it meant we were halfway there. And we were right on schedule.

Maggie was still homesick, of course. Before, the other birds still talked to her. But now they were getting annoyed. They weren't being mean, but they were kind of ignoring her, not looking out for her the way a flock should.

She was flying way at the back when Doc spotted an interesting rock formation. He pointed and we turned the trikes to go and have a look. Big mistake.

What we didn't know was that an eagle had this particular rock wall staked out. He thought it belonged to him, no trespassing, keep out. What the eagle didn't know was that we were only passing through.

Not that I blamed him. Here he was looking at seven of the largest birds he had ever seen, along with two sky trikes, invading his backyard. He knew he couldn't fight all of us, so he decided to make an example out of Maggie.

I saw the eagle first, before Mom or Doc or even the other birds saw him. He seemed to dive in out of nowhere, straight down, heading right for Maggie. There wasn't time to do anything but scream. Which I did.

Since I was sitting in the trike right behind Mom, she practically jumped out of her seat. Our trike did a little hop.

"Good thinking, Eliza!" Mom said, when she'd recovered and seen how my scream had thrown the eagle off course. It probably threw Maggie off too. But either way, the eagle missed. It dived right by her, heading straight down.

Maggie made a sharp turn and tried to get away while the eagle flew below her.

"Go, Mom!" I yelled, pointing at the space between the birds. She banked the trike and turned Maggie's way, trying to put us between her and the eagle.

We weren't fast enough.

The eagle got around our trike and headed for Maggie again. She beat her huge wings hard to get away.

"Hold on!" Mom called out, and hit the gas. We burned a streak across the sky chasing after them. Twice we managed to head the eagle off, but each time he came back around. He was mad and determined to teach Maggie a lesson.

I think if we could have kept going a little longer we might have sent that eagle packing. But there was a problem with the flock. The other birds had scattered. Mom was talking to Doc through a radio in his headset, and Doc was telling us to turn back. Mom gave me a worried look over her shoulder.

"Sorry, sweetheart," she said, "another one of Doc's rules, I'm afraid. The flock must come first."

I hated to admit it, but I knew Doc was right. If we didn't get the flock back together, we risked losing them all. It was a hard decision, but there was really no choice. We had to turn back.

I was watching Maggie for what I thought would be the very last time. She disappeared into a cloud, with the eagle still after her.

"Go, Maggie," I said. "Go!"

Chapter 4

Mom had thought to turn on the camera attached to the helmet during the eagle attack, so we were able to watch it afterward in the Commvee. We hoped it might have captured more than we saw, and maybe we could tell if Maggie got away, but the film showed exactly what we remembered. The clip, I was sure, would be interesting for Mom and Dad's television show, but watching it again made us all feel worse. I could hardly sleep.

Where could Maggie have gone?

I'd already convinced myself that she'd gotten away from the eagle. But then what?

I was lying on a cot outside the Commvee so I could look at the stars and the moon. It was a beautiful sky and I liked thinking Maggie was looking at the same sky too. It was so peaceful. And I was so sleepy.

I had a dream that Maggie was flying right over me. I could see her shape, dark against the moon. My eyes opened and the picture of her against the moon was crystal clear.

"Maggie?"

Whoop!

"Maggie!" I shouted.

She really *was* flying right over us! "Darwin!" He was fast asleep beside me. "Wake up!"

"Mmm?" Darwin blinked and rubbed his eyes. "Eliza?"

"I just saw Maggie!" I told him. I wanted it to be her more than anything.

Who else could it be? I asked myself.

"She flew right over us!" I told Darwin. "But she couldn't see the trikes! Come on, we've got to find her!"

I pulled on my dress and sneakers and scanned the sky with my flashlight.

"I'm coming," Darwin said. "But we'll need sustenance!" He ran back and reached into his sleeping bag to get his favorite snack, a bag of Cheese Munchies.

"Hurry up, Darwin," I said. I pointed the flashlight between us while he caught up.

"I know she was looking for the trikes," I told Darwin. "I wish we didn't have to hide them." We were running down a path through the grass in the direction I thought I'd seen Maggie go.

"Most unfortunate," Darwin said. "Perhaps we'll find her. But then, if we don't, maybe it means she's gone ahead. Maybe we'll see her in Canada."

"She may not know to keep going all the way to Canada. She might stop somewhere before she gets there. She could stop in Montana. Or North Dakota. Who knows?"

"Well, they're nice places too."

"Not if you're a whooping crane. They have airports and power lines and all kinds of hazards. Doc only stops at farms where people know the cranes are coming, where we can look out for the birds. No airports. No power lines. You can't be a crane and act like it's still the year 1800 and plop down anywhere you want. It's too dangerous."

"What if she went back to Texas?"

"I'm not too worried about that," I said. "She may be homesick, but something inside her is still saying, 'It's spring, and it's time to go north.' She'll go in the right direction, just maybe not all the way."

"Watch out, there's a creek," Darwin said. The prairie grass stretched out in every direction, making it look like there was nothing around for miles. But it was full of surprises. Creeks and potholes where water sprang up from underground. Small animals scurrying through. There was a faint light on the horizon, and the birds were starting to appear, balancing on thin stalks of grass that looked like they could barely hold up a bug.

"Let's follow it," I said. "Maggie likes water. And it'll feel good to soak my sneakers." The sun was coming up, and the sky was turning into a huge blue bowl over our heads.

"I wish this creek wasn't so cold," Darwin complained as he stepped into the water. "And I wish it wasn't so wet."

It was still early spring, and the water was mostly melted snow. It was so cold that it stung my legs as if it had claws. It was moving fast too. "Be careful, Darwin, it's a lot deeper than it looks," I said. "It's . . ."

Too late. Darwin lost his footing, and

the current swept him away. "Help!" he cried.

"Hold on!" I said.

"To what?" he yelled.

"I don't know!" I yelled back. Now I was in the current too.

It looked like Darwin was going to get snarled in a tangle of branches hanging over the water.

"Duck!" I yelled.

"I don't see any ducks!" he yelled back.

Then he saw the branches and went underwater just in time. I spotted a log that was turning in a whirlpool and grabbed an end. The current pulled me and the log downstream after Darwin. "Hop on!" I screamed when I got close.

The next thing I knew, we were both riding it down the rapids like a whitewater canoe.

"This creek keeps getting bigger!" Darwin yelled.

I looked behind us. Other creeks were rushing and joining ours. It was turning into a regular river.

"Just hold on!" I shouted.

Down we went, shooting the rapids, playing bumper cars with rocks. It was cold. I was ready to lose my grip when finally I saw a gravel bar ahead.

I pushed off a rock, giving it all I had. The log pitched over and plowed into the gravel, and we tumbled onto the stones.

"Nice work, Captain," Darwin said, rubbing his head.

Shivering, we climbed along the gravel bar and back onto the riverbank. Then I searched the ground for some dry driftwood. Using my glasses as a magnifying lens, I focused a pinpoint of light on a chip of wood until it started to smoke and finally burn. Soon I had a little fire going, and we huddled over it.

About an hour later we were warm and

dry. Darwin actually smiled. I knew that it wouldn't be long before our treacherous ride would turn into a funny story we would remember and laugh about later.

We still had one big problem. Where were we? The creek we'd fallen into was only a tiny part of this river.

"Darwin, give me your honest opinion," I said. "Look upstream. See where the river splits? Did we come down on the left, or on the right?"

"I'm sure we came down on the right," he said.

"I was afraid you were going to say that," I said. "Because I'm sure we came down on the left."

"No, I'm pretty sure we came down on the right."

"I think it was the left."

"At least we agree on something," I said.

"You mean that we're lost?" Darwin said.

"Exactly."

Not only that. Darwin's Cheese Munchies were soggy.

We shared them anyway.

Chapter 5

I wasn't as worried about us as I was about the rest of my family.

I knew Darwin and I were okay; they didn't.

Mom was going to get up first, notice I was gone, and then I could imagine what would happen after that.

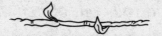

Back at the Commvee, my mom gets a funny feeling. She knows something is wrong. She checks on Debbie and me and discovers my empty bed. She remembers I slept outside, so she calls my name out the door and waits for an answer. There isn't

one. My cot is empty and Darwin and I are long gone.

"Nigel," she says, shaking my dad, who is still asleep. "Get up, I can't find Eliza."

My dad's eyes pop open and he sits up. "What?"

"Eliza is not in her bed. I didn't see her outside, either."

My dad frowns. "She has to be somewhere. She can't just disappear. At least, I don't think she can—but she is remarkably talented. . . ."

"Nigel, wake up," Mom says. She's dressed now. "Of course, she hasn't disappeared." Dad rolls out of bed and changes out of his pj's into cargo pants and a safari shirt. Mom goes to wake up Debbie.

Debbie's not an early riser.

"She'll be back, Mom," she mumbles under the covers. "Check the creek. She's probably baby-sitting the dodos."

Mom pulls the covers off her. "March."

It doesn't take them long to figure out that Darwin and I are nowhere around. We're not with the trikes or the cranes.

"I think they're looking for the missing crane," my dad says. "It was all my fault. I shouldn't have given up on Maggie and the eagle. If I'd recovered her, Eliza would have had no reason to embark on this futile and dangerous search."

"It isn't your fault, Nigel," my mom says. "I'm the one who encouraged her to ride the trikes and spend time with the birds. If I'd done a better job of warning her about the dangers of this trip, she would have been more careful."

Debbie shrugs. "Well, I didn't do anything wrong."

Doc organizes everybody into a line search. He spaces them out along an imaginary line. Then they all walk in the same direction, searching as they go. They circle the camp once and then circle around that circle. *The third time around, Debbie spots something Darwin dropped—some Cheese Munchies. Mom marks the spot with her kerchief, and they search out from there until they're so far from camp, they can only see the brightly colored wings of the ultra-lights.*

"Perhaps we should take the trikes up as well as searching on the ground," Dad says.

"You and Doc go ahead," Mom says. "Debbie and I will keep looking for clues."

When Dad and Doc get back to camp, they find a truck parked by the trikes. The sides are painted with advertisements: SEE THE SPOTTED OWL. PET THE MINK. FEED THE TREE FROG.

Just as Darwin predicted, Colonel Coyote has found our camp. He's standing outside his truck, looking at the trikes.

"Excuse me," Dad says. "May we help you?"

Colonel Coyote turns around and sticks out his hand. "Why, you must be the famous

Nigel Thornberry!" he says. "What a pleasure to meet you. Colonel Coyote's the name!"

Dad grins politely and shakes hands. Colonel Coyote's large brown dog growls from the cab of his truck.

"Hush, Boo Boo," the colonel says.

"What can we do for you, colonel?" Doc says. He's standing off to the side with his hands on his hips.

"Not a thing," says the colonel. "I was just driving through and recognized your camper. Did you know I met some other members of your party the other day? Your daughter and I nearly ran each other off the road!" He turns to my dad. "Just wanted you to know what a fan I am. Your show is a great inspiration to me, you know."

Dad looks at the Endangered Species Museum truck and frowns. He doesn't like the thought of Nigel Thornberry's Animal World encouraging somebody to run an animal

sideshow. "I am certainly not in favor of keeping endangered animals locked up in cages," he says.

Colonel Coyote looks back at his truck. He's heard that complaint so many times that his answer comes out automatically. "I assure you that no animal is harmed in the production of our program." Then he smiles wider. "I take good care of my little stars."

"Maybe you don't harm them," says Doc. "But are you really taking good care of them by forcing them to live cooped up in the back of a truck?"

"Think of how safe they are from predators," Colonel Coyote says.

Doc frowns. He's got a rule about that one, for sure. "There are two kinds of predators," he says. "The animal kind, and mankind."

Dad tries to cut the conversation short. "It has been very nice meeting you, Mister, ah, Colonel Coyote, that is," he says. "Now, *if you'll excuse us, we're rather busy . . ."*

"Lost one of your whoopers?" Colonel Coyote says.

The question takes Dad and Doc by surprise. How does he know? But this makes Dad think Colonel Coyote has seen Maggie. And if he has, my dad is thinking it could be a clue to finding me.

"Yesterday," Dad admits finally. "She was chased off by a rather angry eagle. Have you seen her?"

The colonel shakes his head. "No, but I heard you talking about her on your headsets. I was picking it up on the truck radio. I'd be happy to find her for you, though!"

Dad winces at the thought of Maggie in the hands of Colonel Coyote. He doesn't like the way Colonel Coyote makes it sound like they're working together all of a sudden.

Colonel Coyote would like nothing better than to be on my dad's "team." What a great comeback to people who criticize him for running an animal show.

"No need to trouble yourself," Dad says, trying to steer him away from the idea. "Rather than, ah, 'bringing her in,' you might simply tell us if you see her. She'll come to the ultralights. In fact, she's probably looking for us right this minute."

But Colonel Coyote isn't giving up so easily. "The important thing is to work together," he says. "I'll check the fire roads while you search from the air. Where is Mrs. Thornberry, by the way? She should be getting some of this on film, don't you think?"

Dad gets a horrified look on his face. Doc comes to the rescue.

"Colonel Coyote is right," he says. "If we split up, we could cover more ground. Why don't you head that way." Doc points in the wrong direction, away from where Debbie found Darwin's Cheese Munchies.

"That makes sense," he says. "You can be sure I'll keep a sharp eye out for your missing bird. Does she have a name?"

"Eliza calls her 'Maggie,'" my dad says without thinking.

"Maggie, what a charming name," says the colonel. "And who is Eliza?"

Dad grinds his teeth. He wishes he hadn't mentioned my name. "My other daughter," he answers.

Colonel Coyote looks around the camp expectantly.

"She's out . . . looking for Maggie," my dad explains.

"The more the merrier!" the colonel says. "Don't worry, we'll find her!" Meaning Maggie, of course.

"I dearly hope so," Dad replies, meaning me.

With a happy grin and a wave Colonel Coyote climbs into his truck. A spotted owl is in a cage on the front passenger seat beside him. "It's my lucky day," he tells the owl. "All I need is a whooping crane and a newspaper reporter. We'll get a picture of Nigel and me and the missing whooping crane for the papers, and we'll all be famous together. I can see the headlines now: COLONEL COYOTE HELPS NIGEL THORNBERRY FIND HIS WHOOPING CRANE!"

As soon as Colonel Coyote leaves, Dad and Doc take off in the trikes. They buzz over Mom and Debbie. Mom takes the two-way radio from her belt and presses the talk button. "Good luck," she tells Dad.

They spread out and fly the same kind of line-search pattern in the air that they walked on the ground.

If Darwin and I hadn't fallen into a creek, they might have found us right away. But the water has carried us far away.

We're miles from where they're looking.

Chapter 6

"Water always leads to something eventually," I told Darwin as we walked along the bank of the creek, following it down. "People, a town, something . . ."

A loud noise interrupted me. *Whoop!* My eyes got big. I splashed around a bunch of tall grass bunched along the bank, and there she was, wading up the creek.

"Maggie!"

I told Darwin water would lead us to something—but I had no idea it would be Maggie!

"Eliza?" She couldn't believe it either.

"We've been looking all over for you!" I said. I ran up and gave her a big hug. She hugged me back with one wing. The other one was scraped, slightly bent, and had some feathers missing.

"I got away from that eagle," she explained, "but not without a fight."

I looked at her wing and moved it gently.

"I don't think it's broken," I said. "But I can understand why you were walking instead of flying. But wait a minute, didn't I see you flying over our camp this morning?"

Maggie shook her head. "Not me," she said.

I gulped. Suddenly I felt kind of silly for dragging Darwin into the wilderness after a bird that wasn't even ours. There were a few wild whooping cranes out there migrating on their own. I had just assumed the one I'd seen was Maggie. I gave Darwin a look that said "sorry."

He shrugged. "At least we found Maggie," he said.

Since we found Maggie, all I cared about now was finding our way back to camp. Maggie needed bandages on her wing soon, or it would take much longer to heal. I told Maggie my plan. "If we follow this creek downstream long enough, we're bound to find some kind of help," I said. Maggie looked doubtful.

"If you mean go that way," Maggie said, pointing with her good wing downstream, "I've already been there. Come on, I'll show you."

She led us up the bank to a high place where we could see more sky. The way I had been planning to go was dark with big gray clouds. They looked like they were dragging on the ground.

"A storm's coming," Maggie said. Lightning flashed in the clouds behind her.

The storm was so far away, I could

barely hear the thunder. But I could tell it was going to be a big one. "Okay," I said. "We'll just have to wait it out."

Finding a good place to do that was the question. I could hear the thunder growing louder, and the sky darkened. We climbed farther away from the creek and saw a wild turkey running toward us. "Storm's coming, storm's coming!" he yelled. "Wait!" I said, but the turkey didn't stop. "Do you know where we can go to stay dry?" I called after him. "Over there! Over there!" he said and disappeared around a rock. A crack of thunder boomed overhead. We hurried after the turkey.

"We'd better find shelter fast. I can't take another soaking!" Darwin exclaimed.

"My wing feels really sore," said Maggie in a small voice.

"Look!" I said. Following the turkey had led us to an area with rocks full of weathered caves and overhangs. We found a nice roof of granite we could sit under. For a while we just sat and listened to the thunder.

Finally Darwin broke the silence. "I miss my Cheese Munchies," he said mournfully.

I patted him on the shoulder. "I miss them too," I said. "They were so good, weren't they?"

"So cheesy," Darwin said.

"Even after they got soggy, they were delicious," I agreed.

"I still have the bag," Darwin said. He opened his hand where it was folded into a little square. "I didn't want to litter." He unfolded it and flattened it on his knee.

"Poor Darwin," I said.

Maggie sniffed. "I miss Texas," she said.

I turned to her. "Poor Maggie," I said.

"Yes, poor Maggie," Darwin said. "What do you miss about Texas?"

"Everything," Maggie said.

Darwin stared at the empty Cheese

Munchies bag. "I know exactly how you feel," he said.

"I miss the way the sun rises over the Gulf of Mexico," Maggie said. "I miss the ranch. I miss the other animals—the horses and the cows. I even miss the cat."

"That sounds nice," I said and patted her good wing. For a minute I thought she was going to cry.

I remembered something my mom told me: When one person is brave, it rubs off on others.

"It's going to be okay," I told Maggie. "Just remember that in the fall, you'll be going . . ." But before I could finish, the rain swept in. It poured hard and the thunder sounded like explosions nearby.

We sat and shivered, waiting. It would be dark soon, and we would get hungrier and colder. I tried to stay brave, though. I huddled close to Darwin and Maggie, and we watched the storm in silence as it moved over our area like a gray curtain closing down on us.

I started thinking about being with my family in the warm Commvee. There was a strange, sad feeling inside of me that was sort of hard to explain. I thought about my bed. I thought about Debbie falling asleep with her nose in a copy of *Teenage Wasteland* magazine. I thought about Donnie snoring, and Mom and Dad talking quietly in the next room. I missed them all, really bad. It was almost painful. How long would it take to find our way back?

I was homesick.

Chapter 7

"Is that a real sound I'm hearing, or am I becoming delirious?" Darwin asked.

I wasn't paying attention. I was too busy missing the Commvee and the rest of my family and being homesick for the first time in my life. Maggie hadn't heard it either. I guess her mind was on Texas.

But now that Darwin mentioned it, I did hear a buzzing sound. It was faint and far away, but it was definitely real.

"I think it's a plane!" I said.

For a second I thought it was one of the trikes. But the sound was too deep. We searched the sky. I thought I saw something and then I didn't—then Maggie pointed it out.

An airplane—a forest service *search* airplane!

It zoomed right over our heads. "Hey, we're over here!" I yelled. Darwin, Maggie, and I rushed into the open and waved our arms, trying to get some attention.

"It's gone," I told Darwin and Maggie finally.

"Look," Darwin said. "It's coming back." The plane had turned around to make another pass.

When it went over the second time, I saw the wings waggle. It was a signal from the pilot. He'd seen us. There was no place for him to land, but he could send help.

About an hour went by, the rain completely stopped, and then I heard something that sounded like a mosquito.

It reminded me of Doc's ranch, when Mom and Dad were learning to fly. It sounded like an ultralight.

Wait a minute, I thought, listening hard. It is an ultralight!

"Darwin!" I whispered. "Listen!"

Maggie heard it too. They were coming.

"That plane must have radioed our location to Mom and Dad!" I said.

Then came another sound—the whooping cranes.

Suddenly they were all there. Two trikes and a flock of big white birds cruised right over us.

Darwin and I waved and shouted. But Maggie was the one who got their attention first, with her whooping cry. They circled around. Dad waved and I saw him making a call on his radio. I knew Mom must be close by in the Commvee.

Two light beams appeared over the top of the bank. It was the Commvee! "Mom!" I yelled as we climbed up to meet them. She got out and gave me a big hug.

"I've been so worried about you!" Mom said. She was smiling, but her eyes looked like she might cry. "We guessed you went off to search for Maggie. I should have scared you more!" she said.

"No, Mom," I told her. "You did a better thing by teaching me how to be brave."

Donnie danced around me and babbled happily, then wrapped a bear hug around Darwin and slobbered on his cheek. Darwin forced a smile.

Even Debbie rushed up and hugged me. "We've been looking everywhere for you! We turned the camp inside out, we searched the countryside for miles around. And you know what's really gross? I was totally sweating! But now here you are!" Debbie had tears in her eyes. "This is so intense!" she said, finally.

I looked up at the good old Commvee and thought how great it was to be home. Inside, it felt clean and bright. Mom was

behind the wheel. Debbie and I were sitting behind her. Darwin was crashed out on the floor, and Donnie was bouncing in my lap. Maggie had found a place for herself in the front passenger seat. She'd ride there the rest of the way, while her wing healed.

"Your dad and Doc are leading the flock back to camp in the ultralights," Mom told me. "It'll take us a little longer, but eventually we'll meet up and finish the migration together."

"I'm sorry we got lost, Mom," I said. "We weren't going far. Then we fell in a creek, and we kind of got swept away."

"We had everybody on the planet looking for you," Debbie said. "The firefighters, the police, the national guard, the highway patrol—even that weird guy, Colonel Coyote. Oh, I forgot. You don't know about him."

I shook my head, pretending I didn't know a thing. Debbie didn't know that I knew all about him from Darwin.

"He's this guy who doesn't know how to drive," Debbie told me. "His truck almost ran over the Commvee. Anyway, he's got this traveling road show of endangered animals. It is so lame-o. See the spotted owl. Pet the mink. Feed the tree frog. Those things are painted all over his truck. Is that not bogus?"

"Totally," I said.

Dad's voice came in over the radio. "Come in, come in," he said. "Marianne?"

Mom picked up the dashboard microphone. "I hear you, Nigel," she said.

"We have a slight emergency requiring a bit of assistance from the Commvee," he said. "I do hope you can lend a hand?"

"What's going on?" Mom said.

"There is a vehicle that is apparently stuck up on one of the old fire roads. Perhaps you could see your way up there and help them out, eh?"

"Just tell us the way," Mom said.

"Jolly good!" Dad replied.

"What kind of car is it?" Mom said when he finished.

"It's not exactly a car," Dad said. "More of a truck, I'd call it. You'll recognize it right away. Look for some advertising painted on the side. It says, SEE THE SPOTTED OWL. PET THE MINK. FEED THE TREE FROG."

For a minute Mom didn't say anything.

"Hello?" Dad said. "Marianne? Did you get that?"

"Loud and clear," she said, and put the Commvee in gear.

Debbie and I looked at each other and groaned. Darwin looked kind of stunned too. We were on our way to rescue Colonel Coyote!

Chapter 8

We followed Dad's directions along an old two-lane highway to the fire road. They called it a road, anyway. It was really just two tire tracks up the side of a hill that was normally closed off to everything but emergency traffic. We found a heavy chain with a ROAD CLOSED sign left lying on the ground that should have been blocking the way.

"I guess Colonel Coyote decided to take the shortcut," I said.

Slowly we drove up the hill. It was a bouncy ride over the fallen rocks and around potholes. At last we found it,

Colonel Coyote's truck, with a rear tire wedged into a big pothole. There beside the truck was Colonel Coyote himself, bending over to study the problem.

What made me mad was the way he was dressed. He was wearing cargo pants and a safari shirt just like my dad. Copycat! The nerve.

"Well! Fancy meeting you here!" he said when he saw who it was. At least he hadn't tried to fake my dad's British accent, too.

"You look ridiculous in those clothes," Debbie said.

He gave us a surprised look. "What do you mean?" he said. "They're just like your dad's!"

"That's the point," I told him. "My dad is my dad. And you're not."

"Oh, I know that! But we're a team! Isn't that why you're here?" he said. "Marianne? Tell your daughters we're a team."

"I can't tell them that, because we're

not a team," Mom said. "Nigel spotted you by accident. We're simply here to tow you out and then say good-bye."

"Here, get this on film, will you, please?" she whispered to me. I quietly took out the camera and watched through the eyepiece off to the side as she took out a rope with hooks and attached the Commvee to the Colonel's truck. Then she put the Commvee in reverse and slowly pulled the truck out of the rut, halfway. And stopped.

Colonel Coyote got out and grinned. "A little farther now!" he said. "You've almost got me out! Back up, back up. . . ."

Mom still wasn't moving. She just sat there with a stern look on her face that said "nothing doing."

"Before I finish pulling you out," she said, "you have a little unfinished business with the animals in that truck."

"What do you mean?" Colonel Coyote said.

"I mean it's time to let them go," Mom said.

"Who—what?" Colonel Coyote said. "Impossible! This is the wilderness! How will they live?!"

"They'll live a lot better out here than in the back of your truck," Mom said.

"I refuse to release them," Colonel Coyote said. He planted his feet firmly on the road about six feet away from his truck.

"Well, Mr. Coyote," my mom said. "The forest service will come along eventually and help you out. But either way those animals are going to be set free."

I zoomed in for a close-up on Colonel Coyote. The camera showed him swallowing hard.

"I don't need you to tell me what to do, and I don't need you to help me out of this pothole," he said, and went around the back of his truck. He heaved himself against it, but it didn't budge. His face grew red and then his shoulder slumped. He kicked the tire. "Darn thing!" he said. Then he stood there for a minute, staring at the back of his truck.

"You'll feel good about this later," Mom told him.

"You'll look good too," I said from behind the camera. He turned and finally noticed me. "On film, I mean."

Colonel Coyote's face brightened. "On film? I'm on film?"

"I'll film the whole thing," I said. "You'll look like a true animal lover, setting them free like that."

A strange look came over Colonel Coyote's face. "Animal lover?" he said.

"Oh, absolutely," I said.

"Well, I am, you know," he said, warming up to a new image. "An animal lover, that is. Isn't that right, Boo Boo?" he called to his dog.

The dog hopped out of the cab and snuggled happily against the colonel's leg.

Finally the colonel's hands moved. He swung the rear doors open, and three animals inside blinked their eyes at the bright light. The spotted owl. The mink. And the tree frog.

Colonel Coyote sighed and opened the cages.

"You know, he is good with dogs," I told my mom.

"Maybe he should do something with them," she said.

"Maybe a grooming salon?" I said.

"Well, his own dog could certainly use a bath," Mom replied.

"A grooming salon . . . ," the colonel said. I could see the wheels turning in his head. He liked the idea. "Why, yes! I could work out of my truck! Got a dirty poochie? The colonel comes to you!"

"I'm sure you'd be very successful," my mom said.

Colonel Coyote smiled wickedly. "Oh, yes," he said. "Successful, indeed! I plan on cleaning up!"

And with a cackle he hopped into the driver's seat of his truck so Mom could finish pulling him out.

Chapter 8

Wood Buffalo National Park in Canada looked like a crystal palace in a green garden. The crystal was the ice that was still melting off the trees, and the garden was the green hillside that bloomed with wildflowers. Summer was coming to Canada.

It was beautiful and there wasn't a soul around. I wasn't surprised it took scientists over forty years to find out this was the spot where the last wild whoopers were spending their summers. Some of them were already here.

Our whooping cranes slid in for a landing on an icy pond. They quickly found a

hole and turned it into their own swim-
ming pool.

We found a place to land the trikes and
hike over. By the time we arrived, the
Commvee was there too.

Maggie looked out the window at the
other cranes. I could tell she wanted to
join them. "Why don't you do the hon-
ors?" Mom said, and walked toward the
other birds, leaving me alone with Maggie.

I opened the door and helped her out.
Doc had patched up her wing; she had all
summer to get better, and I knew she would.

"Maybe we'll meet again," I said. "You
never know."

Maggie nodded.

"If you're ever in Canada again," Maggie
said. "Look me up."

"Or Texas," I said.

Maggie looked sad again. I was instantly
sorry I'd reminded her of Texas.

"I'll probably never see Texas again,"

she said. "It's something I'll just have to get used to."

"Don't be silly," I said. "You're going back there in the fall. You're going back there *every* fall. In between spending the summers here."

"I'm going back to Texas in the fall?" Maggie said. She looked stunned.

Oops. "You didn't know that?" I said. "I guess someone should have mentioned it." Although, according to Mom's definition of homesickness, it wouldn't have done much good. Homesickness won't wait. "Migration works two ways," I assured her. "Texas will always be your winter home."

"Now that you mention it, I feel like I could give you directions back to Doc's ranch," she said. She had a sparkle in her eye I hadn't seen before.

"Just remember to turn left at the Black Hills," I said. "And watch out for eagles."

Epilogue

That was the summer Maggie became a real wild whooper. Eventually she would meet another whooper, someone she really liked, and they would start a family.

In the fall the three of them would fly south together. In the spring the family would travel north again. And the whole thing would start again that fall. Again and again, year after year.

I waved good-bye to Maggie out the rear window of the Commvee as our family drove away. We had more travels of our own to do, but for now I was just glad to be home.

Discovery Facts

Whooping cranes are the tallest birds in North America. Adults are five feet tall, about the same size as a preteen human. They choose lifelong mates and produce two eggs per mating season. Right now only about three hundred birds exist in North America. The endangered species is named for its trumpetlike call.

Migration: Many birds move, or migrate, when the weather changes. The main reason is food supply. Whooping cranes, for example, eat fish. When northern rivers turn to ice, they must move south.

Wood Buffalo National Park in west-central Canada was established in 1922. The park is a vast region of forest and plains that covers 28,000 square miles and serves as a summer breeding ground for whooping cranes. Many other animals make their home there as well.

Spotted owls roost near the trunks of pine trees that match their brown feathers. Even in the wild they allow humans to come close.

Minks are related to weasels and ferrets. Unlike those animals, though, minks are semiaquatic—they live and hunt for food in the water as well as on land.

Tree frogs can help predict the weather: They get noisy when a long stretch of rain is on the way. In North America adults are about two inches long.

About the Author

Mark Dubowski has written many books for young readers including other Wild Thornberrys books, Rugrats books, and Salem's Tales. For adventure, he likes hang gliding and wreck diving off the North Carolina coast. He lives in Chapel Hill with his wife (and co-author), Cathy East Dubowski, and their two daughters.